Frederick Brotherton Meyer

A Good Start

Frederick Brotherton Meyer

A Good Start

ISBN/EAN: 9783337410261

Printed in Europe, USA, Canada, Australia, Japan

Cover: Foto ©Andreas Hilbeck / pixelio.de

More available books at **www.hansebooks.com**

A GOOD START

BY

F. B. MEYER, M.A.

AUTHOR OF "CHRISTIAN LIVING," "THE SHEPHERD
PSALM," ETC.

———————

NEW YORK: 46 EAST FOURTEENTH STREET
THOMAS Y. CROWELL & COMPANY
BOSTON: 100 PURCHASE STREET

PREFACE.

THE chapters in this little book might be called "Work-a-day Sermons." They are intended to bring the highest principles of our holy religion to bear on the practical business of every-day life.

Probably all our sermons should have more of this element in them. The Epistles of the New Testament are admirable specimens of the blending of the doctrinal and practical. We are shown how to apply the loftiest principles to the solution of every-day problems. People are not apt to do this for themselves, and like to be shown how to eat and drink, and do all they have to do, in the name of the Lord Jesus, and to the glory of God. This is what these chapters aim to do. They are a piece of undressed cloth — homespun.

One of our greatest modern teachers tells us " *to hitch our wagon to a star.*" And the great purpose of this book will have been amply realized if the readers shall learn the art of linking the simplest actions of life with those eternal truths that burn evermore, as constellations in the firmament.

F. B. MEYER.

August, 1897.

CONTENTS.

I.

A GOOD START.

I.

A GOOD START.

A NEW YEAR is opening before us, and there is some satisfaction in feeling that an opportunity will be afforded of making a really new start. Each true heart in which there is a spark of the Divine life turns eagerly towards the unblemished page, the untrodden way, of the New Year, not with wonder simply, or with hope, but with fervent resolve that the dead past shall bury its dead, and that a nobler, fuller, sweeter spirit shall glisten in the chalice of existence. Years ago, in Leicester, I was accus-

3

tomed to go into the great workshops
and factories with my pledge-cards on
the first day of the New Year, because
it was comparatively easy to induce men
to make a new start with the New Year.
It was in the air.

But it is of little purpose merely to
wish and resolve; let us see whether
there should not be a definite dealing
with mistakes and sins which have lain
at the root of the withered gourds that
represent the years of the past. If once
we could make a new departure in respect to these, there would be some
reason for counting on a permanent bet-
terment for all coming time.

Debt is a fruitful source of misery and
failure. You may owe more than you
may care to tell your dearest friend; you
dare not pass along certain thorough-

fares for fear of encountering individuals whom you have put off with repeated promises that you have not kept; and you hardly dare to open your letters in the morning lest they should contain some stinging remonstrance or threat. Your weekly or monthly wages are pledged before you receive them, and are gone like a flake of snow on the river. All this is very miserable, and must be dealt with. Do not, however, lose heart. Worse troubles than this have been overcome by faith, resolution, and an earnest, sincere purpose.

Take my advice. First, kneel down and confess the sin and mistake of the past to God, and ask his help. Next, put down a list of your entire indebtedness, and make a confidant of wife, or husband, or parent, or friend, not necessarily to gain their pecuniary assistance, but that you may have their sympathy and fellowship. Further, look around your life to see if there is any means of reducing present expenses, or of selling articles of superfluity and luxury in order to reduce your indebtedness. Lastly, make a solemn resolution not to incur a single sixpence of needless expense till every penny you owe is paid. Let this be your new start, and henceforth let it be your rule, to make no purchase and incur no liability which is not easily within your means.

Evil and expensive habits drain away the strength of our lives and becloud the inner horizon. Is it not with the individual as with the state? Supposing it were possible to stay the extravagant expenditure of our people in Drink,

Tobacco, and Horse-racing, would not
squalor, want, and misery, and all their
gaunt tribes, which have settled down on
our vast populations as a horde of Kurds,
fold up their tents, and begone? And,
on a small scale, are not similar evils re-
peating similar ravages on isolated souls,
perhaps on yours? Would it not be an
immense gain in every way, if you were
to give up your Drink and Tobacco, and
employ the money and time which these
consume in procuring books, pursuing
some hobby, planning for a good summer vacation, or engaging in wholesome
and health-giving recreations?

In our schooldays, when running in
matches, we used to begin fairly well
clothed; but as we ran, and found ourselves slowly losing ground, we tore off
one article after another in our anxiety

to reach the goal : and the course was littered with ties, collars, and other articles. Similarly, in the great race of life, the flight of the years should be marked by the weights and sins that we have laid aside. Each new year would be enriched by the needless extravagances we had learned to forego. We should run lighter, breast the stormy waves with less encumbrance, and stand a better chance of getting beyond the rabble that clamor at the mountain-foot, to stand among the rarer spirits on the higher ranges. May I not prevail on you to make some such sacrifice with the opening of the New Year ? It would be a new start indeed !

Bad companions have made havoc with the past. Women who are perpetually dropping in to gossip ; neighbors whose

ways of spending Sunday have introduced a new laxity into your family;
men who talk lightly of God, and women,
and the Ten Commandments. Most in-
sidiously they have been eating away
and deteriorating your nobler life, like
the percolation of water into the cliffs,
which ultimately splinters their strong
sides. The time must come, if you are
to save yourself, when such parasites
must be dropped off. There is no alternative to save yourself from going
farther with them, than to rid yourself
of their society. It may seem hard, but
it is as imperative and urgent as cauter-
izing a bite from a mad dog. With bad
companions dismiss bad books, that leave
a rotten taste, that disincline you to quiet
holy thought, that poison the springs of
love and home. And to the renuncia-

tion of these add all conversation,
pastimes, and places of amusement
which shrivel the soul, as gas does
the plants that wither beneath its
blighting touch. This would be a new
start indeed !

Laxity in your religious life has, without doubt, had something to do with
past failure.   As long as the bright summer sun shines into the forest glades,
the fungus has no chance to flourish;
but when the sunshine wanes, in the
months of autumn, the woods are filled
with these strange products of decay.
It is because we drift from God that our
lives are the prey to numberless and
nameless ills.   Make the best of all new
starts, and returning to the more earnest
habits of earlier days, or beginning them
from now, give yourself to God, believ-

ing that he will receive and welcome you, without a word of remonstrance or a moment of interval. Form habits of morning and evening prayer; especially in the morning get time for deep communion with God, waiting at his footstool, or in the perusal of the Bible, till he speaks to you. Take up again your habits of attendance at the house of God; in the morning and the evening go with the multitude that, with the voice of praise, keeps holyday; and in the afternoon find some niche of Christian service, in your home or elsewhere. Then, inasmuch as you do not wish to be a slip-carriage, which, when the couplings are unfastened, runs for a little behind the express, but gets slower and slower till it comes to a stand, ask the grace of the Holy Spirit to confirm these holy

desires, keeping you true to them, caus-
ing you to be steadfast, immovable, and
set on maintaining life on a higher level.
In all these ways let the new year witness a fresh start.

II.

TEMPERS, AND WHAT TO DO WITH THEM.

II.

TEMPERS, AND WHAT TO DO WITH THEM.

WHAT a shadow is cast over lives and homes by bad tempers! It is Sunday morning, God's day of rest and peace, when the worry and rush of the world should be quiet, and the voices of newspaper boys and hawkers of small wares should be still. A family of little children is waiting to be sweetened and blessed by God, mother, and father. But the mother has become put out over something; she speaks peevishly and crossly, her husband hardly dares put in

15

a word, and the children are scared and talk to one another in whispers. Though there is everything in the pretty home to entrap the sunbeams that play without, a shadow lies over all and mars the day.

Or it is church-time, and the family is late ; the husband and father is waiting, ready dressed, for the house of God, but mother or children are unready, and he calls for them, each time in more irritable tones; and when at last they appear, " Late again," " Always your way," " I am tired and out of patience with you," bring some sharp retort, and the rest of the walk to the sanctuary is either spent in silence, or the parents confine their observations to whichever child they happen to be walking with. What good will the service have after such an introduction ?

How often has a happy day's excursion been spoiled in the same way! It has been the topic of conversation for weeks. The wife has been hurrying all her work to be ready. Such preparations in dress for herself and the children, such cooking of savory tartlets and cutting of sandwiches. The husband has got off for the day with no little planning. Sunshine augurs a happy excursion. But somehow things don't go right. Perhaps the husband is unreasonable and thoughtless, or gives the wife reason to think that he doesn't appreciate her careful provision; or, perhaps, she is over-tired and nervous, and misinterprets a remark meant quite innocently; but one crosses the other, and the ill-natured word, the sour look, the sulking manner, somehow make the whole party miserable — worse than a shower of rain would.

It is impossible to name all the various sorts of ill-temper which vex and curse humanity. The *hot* temper, which flashes out with the least provocation. The *sullen* temper, which is a great deal worse to deal with, because it takes so long to come round. The *jealous* temper, which, in trying to keep all for itself, loses all. The *suspicious* temper, which is always imputing the worst motives. The *malicious* temper, which loves to instil the drop of poison, or make the almost imperceptible stab with its stiletto. Ingenuity has sought to discover analogies to these and other forms of bad temper among the lower orders of the animal creation. This is mulish, and that bearish (with the additional allusion, in this case, to the misfortune of a sore head), and the other is viperish. These comparisons are a little hard on our humble friends and companions in this great Noah's ark. Could they speak, they might say that our sin has introduced the jar and discord into their lives that might otherwise have been peaceful and blessed.

People who have a temper are much to be pitied. They know when it is coming on, or has come, and wish they hadn't yielded, and hate themselves for being disagreeable; yet cannot shake themselves loose from the evil thing that has sprung on them as the jaguar on the antelope, or the ague on the traveller in the tropics. They are disposed, however, to fancy that they cannot help themselves. They have inherited it, as they did the color of their hair, or the shape of their nose. Their mother had it before them, and her father before her. If you want them, you must take them as they are or leave them; and then it is, after all, better to be as they are than like some whom they could name. "I grant you I have a hot tem-per, but then it soon burns itself out, and I am awfully sorry; and as every one must have something, I would rather have this than be unforgiving, or re-vengeful, or stupid." So I have heard people excuse themselves.

Now there is some truth, no doubt, in this talk about heredity. For good or ill, past generations have left their mark upon us; and parents, especially mothers, cannot too deeply ponder it in their hearts. What they are their children

will become; and if there is a strong
taint in the blood, an evil tendency in
any special direction, there is the more
reason why the mother should set herself resolutely to resist it, and replace it
by the opposite. There is no doubt that
this can be done. It has been done in
thousands of instances, and may be
done again.

It is impossible to estimate the value
of good and sunny temper, which goes
through life with a song; looking always
on the bright side of things, and yielding
to the blows of trial and disappointment
with an unfailing grace. It is often associated with a sound constitution and
abounding health, and there is undoubt-
edly a close connection between the
two, but it is not dependent on these;
for, as the great Dr. Arnold testified of

his sister, who was for years a confirmed invalid, but whose chamber was the sunniest room in the house, so suffering and pain have often only set forth to greater advantage the well-spring of sweetness and good-nature which has poured forth like strains of sweet music amid the clatter of a dusty, noisy thoroughfare.

But how may those afflicted with ill-temper be delivered? The Apostle says, "Laying aside all malice, and all guile, and hypocrisies, and envies, and all evil-speakings, as newborn babes, desire the sincere milk of the word, that ye may grow thereby" (1 Pet. ii. 1, 2). That *laying aside* is a remarkable expression, for it means that the thing may be done by one sudden, definite act. We are not to wait till these evil things die down in our hearts, but are to make up our minds, once and forever, to lay them aside; as a beggar his rags when new clothes are offered him. It is a definite act of the *will.* Will you make it now? Will you say, "From this moment I choose to be free of these things, and I deliberately put them off"?

But you fear that this will not help you, you have so often made good resolutions before and broken them. Then take one further step. Trust Christ to keep you. Look up to him and say, "Lord, I have often tried to keep my temper and failed, but from henceforth I entrust its keeping with thee." Expect him to undertake the charge. Every morning look up into his face and say, "I am still trusting thee to be between me and my evil past, and to fill me with thy own sweetness, gentleness, and patience." In moments of provocation dare to trust him still, and to hold to the compact by which your helplessness and evil claim everything from his all-sufficiency. Live thus, and you will become known for the very opposite temper to that which has so often caused you poignant regret.

III.

EXAGGERATION.

III.

EXAGGERATION.

BENEATH all exaggeration there is a basis of truth. When an American said that the whey which flowed from the making of a large cheese in his country was sufficient to run three sawmills; and when another affirmed that the soil of his farm was so prolific that the tendrils of the vine which he had just sown caught him up and entwined around his legs before he could get over the fence, — there was no doubt some truth at the basis of their statements, though only as a drop of homœopathic medicine in a tumblerful

27

of water. And it is this small residuum of truth that veils to the eyes of really good people the evil of this habit. There is no doubt that, in the last analysis, exaggeration must be classed under the head of lying and falsehood. Those that exaggerate are excommunicate from the Temple of Truth.

I heard Mr. Moody say the other day that a lady had come to him, asking how she might be delivered from the habit of exaggeration, to which she was very prone. "Call it lying, madam," was the uncompromising answer, "and deal with it as you would with any other temptation of the devil." A Greater has said, "Let your speech be Yea, yea; Nay, nay: for whatsoever is more than these is of the evil one."

We exaggerate in our narrations. When

a little lad, I had been listening with amazement to the description, given by a lady, of some recent experiences, when my grandfather whispered to me slyly, " All her geese are swans." The words have often come back to me. When mothers describe the excellences of their children, their wit, precocity, and beauty; when travellers narrate their hairbreadth escapes, their marvellous experiences by land or water, all of which end so neatly as to resemble the often polished deal; when ministers give themselves up to tell the story of the crowds they address, the magnitude of their church operations, or the deftness with which they have managed to get their own way, — one is inclined to think that, under the idealizing effect of a strong imagination, geese have become swans.

It seems almost impossible for some
people to tell an unvarnished tale.   The
actual is not wonderful enough.   They
must gild the common sunlight, and paint
the familiar petals of the flowers.   They
think that effect can be produced only by
daubing their canvas with great masses
of gaudy color.   They forget that the
quiet shining of the stars is more healthy
and beneficent than the grandest display
of fireworks that ever poured in cascades,
flashed in wheels, or filled the sky with
ten thousand vanishing fairy lights.   For
my part, I prefer the earlier paintings of
Turner to the later, and the stories of
George Eliot to those of Disraeli or
Bulwer-Lytton ; and I think that most
ordinary people would concur in the
judgment.

We exaggerate in our choice of words.

It is too terrible to hear the young ladies
of the period discussing a panorama of
Alps, a sunset at sea, a vision like that
of Fountains or Clairvaulx under the
soft light of the moon. " Awful," " kill-
ing," " awfully jolly," " too, too, don't-
yer-know," are quite the most refined
and moderate that I need cite here ; one
has no desire to put more of this base
coin into circulation. This pernicious
habit arises in part from ignorance of
the derivation, meaning, and value of
words, but particularly from the desire
to be conspicuous among the little group
around them. Many people mistake big-
ness for greatness, bulk for value. They
resemble the Chinamen in New York,
who buy the largest boots procurable for
their money, under the impression that
in this way they can best obtain their

money's worth.   It is a cheap and easy
manœuvre to hide the paucity of your
ideas beneath the vehemence and loudness of your speech.   This accounts for
a good deal of loudness in voice and
extravagance in phrase.

*We also exaggerate in our religious
phraseology.*   In certain prayers we are
wont to hear, there is gross exaggeration
in the confessions of sin.   If all that some
men say of themselves in prayer be true,
they certainly deserve to be put out of
the church, or be interviewed by their
ministers.   But if you were to take them
at their word, and refuse to allow your
families to associate with theirs, or with-
draw your custom from their stores, on
the ground of their confessions of de-
pravity, they would be very much sur-
prised.   Many a man would threaten to

knock you down if you applied to him the epithets he applies to himself.

So with expressions of love and devotion to the Saviour. We often hear him addressed in prayer in the most familiar and luscious terms. The tenderest, loveliest names are addressed to him. Of course, where these are flowers gathered from the garden of a holy soul, they are fragrant and delightful, awakening the dull sense, and quickening the flagging zeal of all who hear; but where they are far in advance of the evident personal experience, and are contradicted by the behavior of the utterer, as he forces his way into the tram-car from the drenching shower in which the meeting closes, — you feel that there is an air of unreality and extravagance in the whole thing, which must have a terrible effect on him, while it reacts on others like the heavy air that has fanned acres of poppies.

Exaggeration infects all our life. The bride exaggerates the number and value of her presents. The tradesman's advertisements announce that he has 10,-000 bedsteads on view, when he has only 1,000 at the most; that he can offer 1,000 cheeses to choose from, when, with great difficulty, he can get 100 into his cellar; that he is selling off at an alarming sacrifice, when all in the trade know that he is making large profits.

The minister says there are hundreds in his congregation, when, if heads were reckoned, it would be found that there were only four or five score, of whom several were children. Most of us are adepts at drawing the longbow. We are not content with the reflection cast by

events on the plain glass of truth, but
distort them by the convex or the con-
cave, like the two mirrors which are sometimes placed outside eating-houses to
show the effect of a good meal on the
face.

This habit may be traced to childhood.
The simplicity and naturalness of babe-
life is rapidly becoming a thing of the
past. We force the growth of heaven's
nurselings, encourage them in smartness
and old-fashionedness, tell them extravagant fairy stories, rear them in artificial
gaslight, and then complain that they
have lost the sweet ingenuousness of
youth, and grown into young men and
women of the period before they have
barely reached their teens. It is as if
nature should rush into summer without a spring, or the day spring into

the glare of noon without morning.   We
must begin building the Palace of Truth
in the earliest impressions of the nursery.

We should accustom ourselves to think
and speak accurately.   Nothing so tests
the quality of our minds as our use and
choice of adjectives.   When people know
all your adjectives they have come to the
end of your treasures.   It is partly due
to our slovenliness in observing and
describing that we exaggerate in our
speech ; and the evil would be remedied
if young people would read the best
poetry with careful discrimination, asking why Browning or Tennyson uses
such a word in such a connection.   It
is specially valuable, with this object, to
translate some foreign author — Homer,
Virgil, Dante, Racine, or Schiller — find-

ing an English equivalent for each word, though it consume an hour of thought and research.

Let us, also, in describing anything in which we have taken a part, remember that God is listening, and be on the watch against the natural tendency of our tongue to take its coloring matter from the gorgeous palette of the imagination rather than from the neutral tints of sober fact. Let us ask the Spirit of Truth to set a watch upon the door of our lips, allowing nothing to pass out on which he cannot set his seal. Whatever we do, in word as well as deed, let us do all in the name and for the glory of Jesus. Why should we seek to attract the attention of men to ourselves, when to do so may detract from the glory of his workmanship in our character? And if, in the heat of conversation, we are betrayed into exaggeration, and are reminded of it afterwards by the Holy Spirit, let us at once make application for cleansing in the precious blood, and confess to others the wrong we have done to the sacred majesty of Truth.

IV.

ON FALLING IN LOVE.

IV.

ON FALLING IN LOVE.

No flirting, young people, please! You cannot flit around the flame without the risk of burning your wings; and remember, if these are lost, you cannot get another pair; you may be able to crawl or limp, but you will never again bask in the sunbeams or dance with merryhearted glee in the shadows. In other words, you may play at love-making till you lose the power of loving truly, or forfeit for evermore the right of entrance into love's most holy place. Finally, you may find it impossible to convince an-

other that for once you are in dead earnest, and that the time of love has come
to you at length. There is nothing more
terrible in a woman's life than to discover that she has played make-believe
so long that men treat her only as their
plaything and toy, and think that she
is incapable of the true passion. "I
mean it this time," the flirt says, by look
and manner. "I do not believe you,"
the answer is cast back, whether by man
to woman or by woman to man. "I
have watched you narrowly, and can
count up the hearts you have broken,
the lives you have wrecked. You are a
Siren, whose bewitching music beguiles
to death." "Nay, but I am genuine this
once. I mean what I say." "I do not
believe you ; I do not believe you ; I dare
not trust you."

So, whatever you do, young people,
don't flirt. Never appear to love when
you don't. Never lead another on to
think that you really care when you
are not sure. Never play with another's
affections, for fear you should lead to the
giving of what can never be replaced,
and for which you have given no equivalent. I am old-fashioned enough to
think that a man or woman loves *really*
only once. I know what may be said on
the other side, but you must let me think
so. The cream only rises to the surface
in its full wealth once. The perfect
beauty of the morning vanishes an hour
after dawn. Therefore, you who have
not yet given the one love of your
life, do not let it go until you are
sure that it is not wrongly bestowed.
And you who are seeking the twin-

soul, be sure of your own love before you give a sign.

Some of the happiest marriages I have known have been those in which the man and wife were boy and girl together. They played the same games, got into the same scrapes, roamed the autumn woods nutting, and skated over the winter ice. But not less happy may those unions be which have the romantic interest of love at first sight. It *is* wonderful, this falling in love. A man is going soberly along the path of life, with no particular interest in any one, when suddenly a face, a figure, a voice, crosses his path, and straightway his heart is gone. His ideals are realized, his dreams have taken shape. And from that moment, with that wonderful idealizing faculty, he imputes to that young girl all that the poet in him can imagine, or the artist in him depict. "I don't see anything in the girl," a companion says. But he might, poor pur-blind mortal, as well expect to see what Turner saw in a sunset. Take care, young girl, that you live up to that ideal. I pray you, do nothing, say nothing, to dash it to the ground; it is the most sa-cred power love can wield. Live worthy of it; do not descend to his level, but lift him, lift him to yours. True love is built on respect.

We can never forget that Robert Browning, when in London, was wont to repair to the church in Marylebone, where he was wed, and kiss the very steps on which his bride had stood. What love was his, of which she sings in those matchless Portuguese Sonnets! But what an inspiration for her, or any

woman, to show herself worthy of the
ideal which love flings over her every
movement, her handwriting, the very
trinkets she wears, the books she
reads.

If you may not flirt, you should take
every means of knowing one another.
It seems to me that the practice among
the working-classes, of walking out together before there is any thought of
love-making, is an eminently wise one.
We should hear of fewer ill-assorted marriages among the upper classes, if there
were more opportunities of young men
and women becoming acquainted with
each other than can be presented at a
ball or a crush.   In the United States,
young men can take young girls to
places of public amusement without having their names unpleasantly associated

by gossip. This were worthy of importation into England.

However it is managed, be sure to know something more of man or woman than is given when either is dressed in Sunday best, and clothed in most attractive and persuasive manners. All is not gold that glitters. Some people are like the baskets of strawberries sold in London streets; all the big ones are at the top, and those below are very, very small. Young ladies! I am sorry to say it, but some of the nicest of nice men are the most arrant scamps that ever walked. Do not believe their word, do not entrust yourselves to them, unless you know something more of them than they say of themselves. And, young men, I would warn you not to think that a girl can be judged by her manners in the drawing-room, or at a picnic. Try to drop in in the morning ; make an excuse of calling.   See how she looks in her morning dress ; is it tidy, neat, and suitable ; is she helping her mother with the younger children ; is she pleasant in her behavior to the servants? I had once to choose a wife for a young working-man, and was assured that my anticipations as to the suitability of a certain maiden were justified, because she opened the door of her father's cottage at ten in the morning with her hair tidy, a neat print dress (the sleeves of which were tucked up above her elbows), and soapsuds were steaming all up her bare arms. "She will do," I said to myself.

Notice, when you are with the one to whom you are attracted, these points : How does the young man speak of his

parents? does he call his mother
mother? Does he take an interest in
his younger brothers or sisters? Does
he attend church for himself, or only
because you go with him? Does he
ever suggest taking you into the public-
house, or to some place of amusement
where women are treated with unhal-
lowed familiarity and scant respect?

As a young man acts in any of these
respects, you may judge him; and remember, that little unsuspected words
and acts on his part are more likely to re-
veal his true character than any number
of protestations and vows. Every man
reveals his real self once or twice to the
woman he woos; and if only women
would act on the slight suspicions which
sometimes cross them, how many broken
hearts would be saved!

Do not suppose that you can alter a man after you are wed. If you cannot fashion him before marriage, you cannot after. A woman dreams that when once she is wife, she will be able to mould her husband to her mind. It is a vain illusion, which in millions of cases has been rudely dissipated. Besides which, are we always able to command the co-operation of the Holy Spirit, especially when we have acted in direct violation of his expostulations?

If you are not sure, don't let your heart go, young girl. Break off an engagement rather than expose your wooer and yourself to lasting misery. It will be kinder to him in the end, because where there is not absolute oneness there cannot be lasting happiness. If he threatens to commit suicide, be well assured he will never do it. He has no right to talk to you like that, and is a coward to play upon your feelings. Besides, a man who talks so lightly of throwing away his own life is not one to whom a woman should entrust hers.

Young men had better consult their mothers or sisters before they take the irrevocable step. Women are quick at reading character, and those that love you will be most likely to choose well for you. Let the women of your family into your secret. Dear souls, they will guess your secret even if you do not tell it, and you may as well tell it; it will please them, and they will advise you well.

There is no harm in early engagements. When I am sure that it is a love-match, and in other respects suitable, I am glad to see two young people drawn together, though in their teens. Probably nothing will more certainly keep them pure and sweet amid the contaminating influences of the world. Let them begin early; it does not matter how long the courtship lasts. The courting times are very happy and blessed times, when young hearts are not too full of hopes and plans and anticipations to enjoy the pathway over which they are passing, and cull its flowers. But in these courting days remember that your relationship be kept on the highest level. It must be spirit to spirit, soul to soul. That which begins and ends with the physical will sooner or later land you both in a ditch. Take care!

Beware! The physical must be the sacrament and expression of the spiritual, else it will widen into the rift that makes love's music mute.

Mind that love-making be only in the Lord. Let it be ensphered in the love of God. Then, like the wedding-ring, the beginning will be everywhere, the end nowhere. For a Christian to marry one who is out of Christ is the grossest folly. Not only is there a flagrant act of disobedience to the distinct command of Christ, but there is the additional certainty that sooner or later there will be manifested an incongruity, a disparity, a want of sympathy in the deepest and most sacred subjects. I have had a wide experience, and been admitted into numberless homes, but I have never seen perfect happiness where this distinct command of the gospel has been violated; and I have never met a case in which the believing partner has won the unbeliever, except when faith may have come to the heart of one after marriage.

Lastly, to all who are unwed, I give my fervent advice: Make it a matter of earnest prayer. Let your heavenly Father choose for you. Do not think that life is necessarily a failure if no supreme love enters it. There are very happy and useful lives on every side that have never been blessed with a supreme affection. Live for God. Make him first. Wait on him and keep his way. In his own good time and way he will give you your heart's desire.

V.

ON BEING STRAIGHT.

V.

ON BEING STRAIGHT.

To be straight is to be true. There is no more important exhortation on the page of Scripture, than where the Apostle says, "*Whatsoever things are true . . . think on these things.*" A friend of mine, educated in one of our great English schools, says that the most formative words of his life were addressed to him by his head master, as he said good-by : "*Be true,*" he said, "*always be true.*" My friend records that those words have often come back to him at critical moments of his life, indicating his path as with a finger of light.

Every man, in his heart of hearts, has some knowledge of what is eternally right and good. You see it in the little child who blushes and conceals itself when it has told a lie, or taken forbidden fruit, and who shares its sugar-candy with its little brother. It may be but a dim flicker, but it is there. The radiance that streams through the open door of heaven may have become very faint by the time it reaches the spot on the dark common where you stand, but unless you wilfully turn your back on it, it falls around your feet and on your heart.

Truth, so far as it concerns us, is that attitude of soul which thinks and acts in consistence with its highest ideals. And the marvel is, that as we act consistently with our ideals, they tend to become always nobler and purer, and to approxi-

mate more nearly to those highest stan-
dards which exist in the nature of God.
If a man be true to his better self, he
will become the pupil of the Spirit of
Truth, and catch a glimpse of farther
horizons, so that ultimately he will come
out into the great light of eternity, as it
shines from the face of Christ.

Be true in your speech. Do not say
one thing to a man's face, and another
behind his back. Do not flatter where
you inwardly despise and contemn. Do
not exaggerate as you repeat your pet
stories, for the sake of effect, and to win
a smile. Let your speech mirror your
convictions, so far as may be right and
possible. Let your yea be yea, and your
nay, nay. Do not puff the article you
want to sell beyond its real value, or say
a single word more of it than you can

verify. In the old fable the palace walls were panelled with mirrors, on which a mist arose when insincere and untruthful words were uttered within their precincts; realize that such mirrors are ever around you, and see that you never cause a stain or blur.

Be true in your actions. If you are an artist, portray Nature as you find her, never using your colors for mere effect or display. If you are a mechanic, do not make articles merely for show or sale, but because they realize the purpose they profess, boots to keep the feet dry, clothes to wear, furniture to last. The world is full of shoddy and sham, of scamped workmanship in our houses, of mottled paper that looks like marble, of tinsel that resembles gold, of paste-jewels, and veneer. Do not choose a trade for your boy which is a success in proportion as it is a mimicry and sham. Do not deal in counterfeits, lest you contract the habit of unveracity and falsehood. See that your hands and eyes and heart are in rhythm with your highest conceptions of what is honest, lovely, and of good report. Bear witness, as Jesus did, to the Reality of Things. Did Paul ever make a tent which deceived the purchaser?

Be true in your opinions. We are all liable to be warped in our opinions by considerations of what is popular, expedient, and likely to commend us to our fellows. The statesman is sorely tempted to listen to the wire-pullers of his party, the catch-cries of his constituency, the lead of some popular organ, and to allow these to divert him from the path of conviction and conscience. How often have men like Pilate been led to act against their clear judgment by the insistence and fear of the mob. Like waves of the sea, they are driven by the winds and tossed. Like the weather-vane, they move around with the least puff of breeze. This is specially the temptation of religious leaders, who are assailed by many voices, such as : Will it pay? Will it attract people, or aleniate them ? Will it be popular, or the reverse? Life is pitiable, indeed, when such considerations have to be balanced.

" Better be a dog, and bay the moon ! "

Of course we must speak the truth *in love.* Some seem to think that truthfulness, of necessity, involves rudeness and ruggedness of speech, a rasp on the

tongue, an abruptness in the act. But
this need not be. The King of Truth
was also the good shepherd, whose words
were music, whose ways were mercy as
well as truth, and whose glory comprised,
in equal proportions, truth and grace.

Whatever happens, be true. As you
stand behind the counter, a question may
be asked by a customer about some article you are desirous of selling. An eva-
sive answer, or a slight deviation from the
strict truth on your part, will complete
the transaction. The manager or shop-
walker is listening. Shall you say it?
If you do, no one will be much the
worse. If you don't, you will lose your
situation. What shall you do? Believe
me, there is no alternative. You must
follow your King, the King of Truth.
And if you are cast out, he will receive

you, and count you his companion, and give you a deeper glimpse than ever into his heart.

Or you are beginning to question certain conceptions of truth in which you have been reared. The more you think of them, the more unable you feel to accept them. To renounce them will give pain to those you love, will lead them to look at you shyly, will condemn you to ostracism and misunderstanding. On the other hand, it would be easy to shut your eyes, and sign your name to what all your neighbors hold. But, I pray you, do not do it, or you will put out your eyes as surely as Hubert's hot irons put out Arthur's.

This is why there is so much infidelity in the world. There are evidences enough, not only in books, but in the heart and soul, in life, in the world around. The moonbeam's silver path comes across the mere to the feet of every young warrior, and the hand clothed in samite offers to each the Excalibur sword. For each dreamer, of all the young pilgrims across the wold of time, there waits the angel-ladder. Beside each one of us the bush in the desert burns with fire. The difference between those who see and do not see these things lies in their devotion or disobedience to truth, so far as they know it.

If a man refuses to obey the truth, so far as it is revealed to him, the glimmering light dies out from his soul, and his eyes become dimmed, so that he cannot see.

If, on the other hand, a man obeys the truth, he is like one that had been lost in the catacombs; suddenly stooping down, he touches a cord, which he catches up and follows hour after hour, until it conducts him to the mouth of the long corridor, whence he steps forth into the perfect day.

It may be that some shall scan this page who have no faith in Christ or Christianity. I ask them to follow this simple recipe: Put away all from your life, in speech, thought, or act, which is inconsistent with your highest conceptions of the supremely Right and Good. Then be true to those conceptions, and, as you are, you will find them heighten and widen; you will discover yourself one in a great company, who are all travelling in the same direction towards the rising sun; after a while you will encounter One who speaks of things of which you have become profoundly and experimentally convinced ; being of the truth, you will listen intently to him as he tells of things that lie beyond your view ; but as he spake truly of things in which you could follow him, so you will believe that he speaks truly of these others ; as when he says that God is a Father, that hereafter there is a home for those who trust and love, that he is the only begotten Son, to know whom is to know God, and to follow whom is to have everlasting life. Be straight : be strong : be true.

VI.

ON DOING A GOOD DAY'S WORK.

VI.

ON DOING A GOOD DAY'S WORK.

LONGFELLOW's village blacksmith felt
that "something accomplished, something done," had earned a night's repose; and I suppose that he did little
else than shoe the farmers' horses, or put
new shares to their ploughs; yet he had
the perpetual consciousness that he
was doing something in the world, con-
tributing to its well-being, performing a
necessary part in the machinery of the
village-life. It is not to be supposed
that the honest man did his work for
the money it brought him, but for the

71

love of doing it, the pleasure of minis-
tering, however humbly, to the common weal. However well he were paid,
it would be a source of infinite regret
and shame if his work were superficially
and perfunctorily executed; if a horse
were lamed, because the nail was driven
too far home, or a day's work in the
sowing-time were lost because the share
broke in mid-furrow.

This is the ideal of all good work.
Too many work for the wage to be paid
them at the end of the week, and become so degraded in their aim that they
will only put in the best work when
they are promised the highest pay. Let
the remuneration be second-rate, their
work will be second-rate; let the workshop be a peasant's cottage, their style of
workmanship will lack the finish which

would certainly be put in for a palace
or church. This appraising of our work
by the amount of wage it will bring is
vicious in the extreme, and sooner or
later begets a perfunctory, superficial,
and mean disposition. The man who
reserves his best work for the best pay
will ultimately be content to put in the
semblance of the best work, though it
be a bit of arrant scamping, in order to
secure, as soon as he may, the promised
wage; in this case, however, it should
scorch his hand as the wage of un-
righteousness.

Do you think that the old monks, who
built religiously, and for the eye of God,
stopped to ask whether some curiously
carved stone was intended for the vaulted
ceiling, or the ornamentation of a door-
way through which successive genera-

tions of admiring pilgrims would pass?
It was enough to be permitted to put
one piece of carving in the house raised
for the honor and glory of God; there
must be nothing inferior there, nothing
that would cause the carver shame if
he met the memory of it in any world,
nothing that would seem contemptible
to future generations if it should drop
from its place to lie within the easy
inspection of every passer-by.

Can you imagine a true artist paint-
ing an inferior picture because it would
be *skied* in an exhibition, or sold cheap
at an auction? He would tell you that
he dared not do it. He would be untrue
to his loftiest ideals; if he permitted
himself to fall so low, he would soon lose
his power of realizing his dreams, and
deteriorate into a sorry hack. The ar-

tist's eye would fail to perceive, the
artist's hand to achieve. Nature would
veil her charms from his eye, who sought
them only for mercenary ends.

Would a physician, who was inspired
with the true spirit of his profession,
reserve his deepest insight, his longest
patience, his most skilful treatment, for
the rich, whose golden sovereigns would
freely pour into his banking-account,
whilst the child of the peasant might
take its chance?

And if each of these is expected to
do his work in the world for the honor
of his profession, and the lasting benefit
of men, why should not all men and
women do whatever God has given them
to do for the same high end? Not for
fee or reward, not for the wages which
are, of course, necessary and deserved,

not for the applause and praise of one
or many; but because work is honor-
able and noble, because a true man
finds his highest reward in putting his
noblest self into all he does, because
it is a scandal and shame to be content with anything less than the best,
because God and his high angels are
looking on, and because scamped work
will return on us in other worlds to con-
front and shame us. There is no surer
sign of deterioration of character than
contentment with inferior work.

We are accustomed to speak of our
work as a vocation or calling. Let every
man, says the Apostle, abide in the calling in which he was called. Some are
called to be servants, some to be mas-
ters; some to administer five talents,
others one; but every man is as much

called of God to his life-work as the
minister is called to preach, or the physician to combat disease. Do you expect
these to be above the questions of dol-
lars and cents, there is the same obli-
gation on yourself. Would you think it
mean of the servant of God to preach at
half or quarter power if he were to receive but a trifling solatium, or to cease
preaching if he shall have realized a
competence? But are you not guilty of
similar meanness if, in altered conditions, you permit your conduct to be af-
fected by sordid considerations? Some
men are called to sweep chimneys, and
others to be archbishops, but in the
sight of the Almighty there may be less
inequality than we suppose ; and the
sweep will stand highest at last, if he has
driven the soot out of the intricacies of

old chimneys with more eager care and with nobler purpose than the archbishop has administered his diocese.

What counts in God's sight is not the work we do, but the way in which we do it. Two men may work side by side in the same factory or store : the one, at the end of the day, shall have put in a solid block of gold, silver, and precious stones ; whilst the other has contributed to the fabric of his life-work an ephemeral, insubstantial addition of wood, hay, and stubble, destined to be burnt. What is the difference between these two ? To the eye of man, there is none ; to the eye of God, much : because the one has been animated, in the lowliest, commonest actions, by the lofty motive of pleasing God, and doing the day's work thoroughly and well ; whilst the other wrought

to escape blame, to secure the commen-
dation of man, or to win a large wage.
Never be ashamed of honest toil, of
labors, however trivial or menial, which
you can execute beneath the inspiration
of noble aims; but be ashamed of the
work which, though it makes men hold
their breath in wonder, yet, in your
heart, you know to have emanated from
earthly, selfish, and ignoble aims.

What we make, makes us. The slight
gauze on which the mantle of the incan-
descent light is formed flares away in a
moment, but the solid fabric wrought on
it by chemical agents will be luminous
for a thousand hours. So the things
we make in the world pass away as a
wreath of flame, but the motives with
which we do them go to make ourselves
for better or worse. If you do your work

in slovenliness, you become a sloven. If
you do your work perfunctorily, you become a hypocrite. If you work only for
the eye of man, the sense of God will die
out of your life.

Men fret, for instance, at being tied
to a clerk's desk. Surely, they say, any
one could direct these envelopes, copy
these letters, cast up these interminable
columns ; and in their contempt for their
life-work they fail to see that its very
unimportance is giving them a better
opportunity of cultivating punctuality,
patience, fidelity, and similar passive vir-
tues, than they would have if they played
a more conspicuous part in the world's
life, or in spheres where certain other
considerations nerve to supreme efforts,
which, in their case, can only be called
forth by lofty principle.

At the end of life's brief day we shall be rewarded, not according to the work we have done, but to the faithfulness with which we have endeavored to do our duty, in whatever sphere. Let us live and work with that day in view ; and let us never forget that the ultimate reward for conspicuous service will be given not to the one who seemed, to the eye of man, to render it, but to those also who enabled him to render it.

The servant who prepares my food, or saves me the necessity of doing the many duties of my home, thus setting me free to write, or preach, or minister to men, will, in God's reckoning, be credited with no inconsiderable share of the results of anything which may have been achieved through my endeavors. The great deed that blesses the race seems to be wrought by one, but it is really the result of the contributed quotas of scores and hundreds of unnamed and unnoticed workers; and these, in so far as they entered into the spirit of his labors, shall share the reward. Those that sow and those that reap shall rejoice together.

This is the way to do a good day's work. Begin it with God; do all in the name of the Lord Jesus and for the glory of God; count nothing common or unclean in itself — it can only be so when the motive of your life is low. Be not content with eye-service, but as servants of God do everything from the heart, and for his "Well done." Ask him to kindle and maintain in your heart the loftiest motives; and be as men that watch for the coming of the Master of the house.

VII.

SAVORLESS SALT.

VII.

SAVORLESS SALT.

No wonder that the common people hung on Christ's words. He was a Master of the Art of Illustration, because he sought his emblems, not from remote corners of creation, or its recondite processes, but from the common incidents of ordinary human experience. Salt and light, birds and lilies, gates and roads, trees and their fruit, houses and their foundations. But there was more than art. He knew the hidden secrets of creation, and could tell the heavenly pattern upon which everything was fashioned.

And how full of encouragement he was! He was so willing to give men credit for their best; and in doing so, summoned to view qualities, the existence of which their possessors had never dreamed, or encouraged them to continue in paths on which they had ventured with hesitating steps. It was not a small encouragement to these humble peasants and fishermen to be told that they were capable of checking the evil that was eating out the vitals of society around them, as salt stays the progress of corruption. Have we ever realized sufficiently, or used, this antiseptic power with which all good men are invested?

It is a sad comment on society that it needs salt. You do not think of salting life, but death, to keep it from rotting.

This, then, was Christ's verdict on the society of his time. It had enjoyed the benefit of all that Greek intellectualism and Roman government could effect, and yet was like a carcass on the point of putrefaction. But is not this the state of all society from which religion is banished, or where it has become a system of rites and dogmas? Go into any large workshop or counting-house or public-house, where men feel able to talk freely, and there is too often the smell of the charnel-house in the stories that pass round, and the jokes that pass from lip to lip. The absence of *ladies* is supposed to give a certain amount of license, as if *gentlemen* had no special squeamishness.

Here is something that each of us can do. Perhaps we cannot speak; we cannot

shed a far-reaching ray of light to warn
from the black rocks, and guide to har-
bor ; we seem shut away from scenes of
Christian activity, but we can be good
salt, checking the evil which would otherwise infect the air of the world, and
breed disease in young and healthy
lives.

The salt has just to be salt. It need not
attempt to be a voice, a spark of light, or
a thrill of electricity. Let it just be good,
wholesome salt, and quietly, unobtru-
sively, it will fulfil its great mission. A
little child has often arrested the commis-
sion of a horrid crime, with its innocent
look and its trembling, tearful face. A
gentleman who travels much among
lonely farmhouses told me the other day,
that whenever a fierce dog ran barking at
him, he stooped down, and looked it in

the face; and he said that he had never
met a dog yet which could stand a steady
gaze; so there is something in the look of
a really good man that abashes sin. The
presence of a Henry Martyn has turned
an East Indiaman from a floating hell
into a very paradise. The look of a Fin-
ney has stayed the blasphemy of a large
factory, and brought all the mechanics
to their knees. Billy Bray's life purified
a whole district of Cornish miners. In
fact, it would be impossible to tell of all
the prisons, the backwoods settlements,
the soldiers' camps, the slave planta-
tions, where the progress of sin has been
arrested, and the devil himself has slunk
abashed to his lair, before the presence
of a resolute genuine man of God. *You*
might do the same, only you must be a
genuine character. Salt must be good

before it can effect its great preventive ministry. But if it is good it will do it. And if you really are full of the Holy Spirit, and of faith, your very presence will be all that is needful to stay the evil that cries to Heaven.

When I was in Liverpool, the women of a large reformatory ward broke into open rebellion, expelled their warders, barred the windows and doors, and gave themselves up to every species of indecency. The authorities were nonplussed, and could not tell what to do; but Mrs. Josephine Butler volunteered to go alone, still the disturbance, and bring these poor lost creatures back to decency. The extreme difficulty and danger of the task were set before her; but she persisted in her request, and finally carried her point. As soon as she appeared, she was met

with a yell of madness; but the uproar
at last subsided, that outburst of un-
womanliness died down before the spell
of her sweet and holy presence, and
presently she opened the doors, and admitted the warders.

But good salt will be pungent. It has
a savor about it which bites and stings
whenever it comes in contact with an
open wound. If you are holy, just, and
faithful with a true man, he will evince
no feeling of annoyance; but if with a
vicious man, he will splutter, make a wry
face, and show violence of hand or foot.
Christ was salt to the Pharisees, and
they crucified him. Joseph was salt to
his brethren, and they put him in the
pit. Paul was salt to his fellow-country-
men, and they arraigned him before the
bar of Cæsar.

But always distinguish between salt and acid. Acid corrodes, burns, kills. Salt smarts, heals, saves. Some rejoice in what they call plain speaking; but they forget to speak the truth in love, and are like a physician who goes around with wholesome but nauseous medicine, and whenever he sees a mouth open pours some down. It is necessary to wash the saints' feet, but be sure you do not do it in scalding water. If you have to tell men that they are the enemies of the cross of Christ, do it weeping. Let it be evident that you had no axe to grind, no selfish end to serve, no grudge to pay, when you rebuke others by life or word for things which ought not to pass unnoticed.

Salt may lose its savor. Housewives tell us that if it be allowed to get damp,

it will lose all taste of salt, and become
quite useless. So we may lose all power
of arresting sin. Yonder is a man who
once stood high in the opinion of the
church and the world; but he committed
one act of inconsistency, and that has
sealed his lips. For him to check others
is like Satan rebuking sin. They turn
and say, Take the beam out of thine own
eye before attempting to take the mote
from ours. Here is another, who has
no power to rebuke, because he is con-
scious of some secret sin, which pro-
duces indecision in his manner. In
another case it is as when Lot remon-
strated with the men of Sodom, and
urged his children to escape. He is
tarred too deeply with the same brush
for them to heed. They ridicule him
as a childish dotard.

You cannot salt salt. You may salt
beef and mutton and pork, and a hun-
dred other substances, but you cannot
salt salt.   If it has lost its savor it is
thenceforward good for nothing; but is
cast out on the street, and trodden under foot of men.   As long as a man has
never passed under the influence of
Christianity you may hope for him ; but
when he has gone into it, and through
it, and come out on the other side un-
saved, there is little to hope for.   He is
fit neither for the land, nor yet for the
dunghill.   He is cast out as almost
hopeless, so far as human judgment
goes, though with God there are limit-
less possibilities.

Let us beware of such a fate, and live
daily such straight, strong, pure, noble
lives that evil may be abashed in our

presence 'and slink away, and that an arrest may be put on the plague that walketh in darkness, and the pestilence that wasteth at noonday. And whatever you do, keep your savor.

VIII.

OUR HOLIDAYS.

VIII.

OUR HOLIDAYS.

WE need to have a pause in the rush of our life, whether by the seaside, on the moor, or in the green nook of the country. As nature needs the repose of winter after the exhaustion of her autumn produce to recuperate herself for the coming spring, so do we need seasons in which our intellectual and physical vigor, to say nothing of the spiritual, may be reinvigorated and renewed. Hence the need for summer holidays. There are certain directions, however, which we should bear in mind, if we

99

would make the most of our annual vacation, which has come to be part of the yearly programme of most people.

Be careful with whom you travel. It is certainly remarkable how amiable people, for the most part, are when they are away from home; that is, if they have got their corner seat, are quite sure that their luggage is safe, and have got the first place for being served at the dining-table. These conditions being granted, it would seem as if the moment people leave their houses they put off all trace of peevishness and irritation, and array themselves in the brightest and pleasantest moods. The little child who asked his father, when going through a cemetery, where all the bad people were buried, might well ask where all the ill-tempered people take

their holiday. It has been observed
that if you meet a party for the ascent
of Snowdon, for a drive on a coach
through the Highlands, or for a picnic
arranged from a " Hydro," you will con-
gratulate yourself on having discovered
the most amiable of mortals.

But if you are planning to spend all
the time with another or others in the
same party, to share with them the jolts
and mishaps, the ups and downs, which
are incident to journeyings at home and
abroad, you should be very careful whom
you select. One who looks on the
bright side of things, who is hopeful
when the morning opens with mist or a
downpour of rain, who can laugh glee-
fully over a misadventure, and enjoy
contentedly the substitution of ship bis-
cuits for ham sandwiches in the lun-

cheon-baskets, with such like mishaps;
one who is capable of reverence amid
the sublimities of nature, and who will
not speak of the roseate hues of morning, or snow with evening pink, as " awfully jolly ; " one who is capable of
being quiet and hushed ; one who, after
the most gleeful frolic, can turn naturally
to thoughts of God, — give me such a
companion for my summer holidays.

Be careful to take a good book with you.
There are many books which we cannot
read in the rush of daily life. It is well
to put one of these in the trunk; not, of
course, a deep theological treatise, or
Balfour's suggested basis for religious
faith, or a manual of social and political
economy, however closely it bears on the
problems of the day. Apart from these
there are books, interesting and sugges-

tive, stimulating thought and quickening imagination, which we can read without fatigue, and to have read which will have made the holiday memorable. There are, for instance, books on natural investigation, works of history, biographies, the highest class of stories. These do not tax the mind unduly, while they give it that delicious sense of exercise which turns the current of the thought into new channels, and leaves a permanent possession of information and interest.

Be careful to think about other people. I am beginning to see that the people who are always making for the best seats do not on the whole fare better than those who wait their time. In any case, the scheming and pushing, the rushing and dashing, the fever and excitement, the uncomfortable sense of having acted selfishly, must deprive selfish folks of the power of tranquil enjoyment. To think about other people is to do the best for yourself. Perhaps if you look after the luggage of that nervous traveller, you may find your own in the van, if you give up your comfortable corner for that little child to go to sleep in, it is as likely as not that the angels who watch it will contrive to put you into a sound slumber; if you will see to others getting refreshment, you will probably think less of your own hunger and fatigue, and there will be your share of the twelve baskets full of fragments. It is remarkable how often a kindness done to a stranger will open his heart, secure you a friend who will show you interesting views of the country through which you are passing, and which you must otherwise have missed.

Be polite and courteous to the servants and natives. I have seen disgraceful things. I remember a Saturday night in Norway, where the people of a quiet inn were preparing decorously for the succeeding day, that a rowdy party of young Englishmen came in and demanded drink, behaved rudely to the modest servant-girls, shouted boisterously to each other, and turned the place into a bear-garden. With what little humanity do many tourists treat the tired servants of the hotels or inn! How vulgarly they speak to the people they meet on the roads, discussing their manners, and commenting on their ways! What a conception must be given of the average life of English people! more fond of a good dinner than of a fine view, inclined to wrangle over their bills, imperious in their demands, certain that money will secure them a right of entrance anywhere. On the other hand, kind words and little courtesies cost nothing, but, like oil, ease the axles.

Be specially careful that the summer holiday should be a time of spiritual refreshment. A Christian man confided to me the other day his regret that he generally came home from his summer vacation worse spiritually than he started; and that it took him several weeks to regain the old position. This arises partly from the occupation of our mind with the outward, with the fresh scenes and people ; and thus our energy is diverted from the interior and eternal.

Then our habits of private and domestic prayer are liable to be broken in upon by the early morning start and the late, tired return. We are compelled to spend our time in the presence of others; and the larger the party, the more impossible to get alone. Then there is the temptation to let ourselves go into lightness of speech and act, partly induced by the exhilarating air, and partly by the flow of high spirits around. From all these causes we are liable to lose the fine tone of our spiritual life, and to get jaded.

To counteract these influences we must get our half-hour, or hour, alone with God and our Bible, though we rise a great while before day. We should have our pocket Bible at hand, that we may turn to the Psalms or the Prophets, as the divine comment on nature. And it

is well to be provided with some helpful
devotional book, the reading of which
will direct our aspirations towards God
and heaven.

To me the vacation is generally associated with reading a book or books of
the Bible thoughtfully, trying to see
deeper into them than before ; and for
many years I have read the Book of
Revelation though at that time.   There
is a special congruity between the splen-
dor of its conceptions and the vision of
ocean, sky, and mountain.   It is well,
when we have witnessed the dawn of
some new revelation, as well as of the
morning; the great deep of God's judgments, as well as the ocean ; the moun-
tains of his righteousness, as well as
Snowdon, Cader Idris, or Mont Blanc.

IX.

HOW TO SPEND SUNDAY.

IX.

HOW TO SPEND SUNDAY.

" A Sabbath well spent brings a week of content."

So the old couplet runs, but the difficulty lies in how to spend Sunday well. Too many seem only proficient in the art of how not to do it. Now I feel able to give some advice on this matter, as the Sundays of my early life were the red-letter days of the whole week; and as I look back on them, the recollection sends blessed thrills of joy through my heart. It is as though the light of those days, their fragrance and dew, lie still in the garden of my soul, where I now walk with the many concerns and added interests of manhood.

The art of making Sunday a happy day, if art there was, on the part of my parents, lay in their sharing its hours with the whole family. There was no exclusiveness, no withdrawing from the general life for selfish purposes, no sign that the children were a bother, to be got out of the way as expeditiously and for as long a period as possible. This is where so many families go wrong. The children are sent off to the nursery to spend the time with servants, who may have little interest in them or religion, or dismissed to the Sunday-school, that the parents may have unbroken leisure for sleep or pleasure. It is the only day in the week I can get for myself, says the father. It is the only day in the week that I can have my husband to myself, says the mother. It is the only opportunity we have of seeing our friends, say both. And so the children are left to their own devices ; and on those Sunday afternoons, however unconsciously, the seeds of bitter harvests are sown. Directly self comes into the first place in the home-life, we begin to prepare for ourselves almost interminable pains in after years. The path of safety and true happiness is in seeking the well-being of those around, from the smallest babe to the most unkempt servant who has come under the shelter of our roof.

A well-spent Sunday must not begin with self-indulgent lying in bed. Of course breakfast may be a little later, and the very essence of a happy Sunday lies in everything being different from

every other day of the week ; but when
the hour has been fixed, it should be kept.
It makes such a difference when the
father, mother, and children are all to
time, and can begin breakfast together.

May I not here put in a strong plea for
family prayers on this, if on no other,
day of the week ?   Where the father is
absent on business, as a commercial, or
before breakfast, as a mechanic, it is not
possible for the whole family to gather
at the family altar ; and there is the
more reason why, on Sunday morning,
the father should take his true position
as head and priest of his house gathered
before God.   Why should not each child
say a text, mother and father and servant
doing the same ?   In one family in Edin-
burgh, where I love to be, the father,
a professor in the University, reads his

verse in the selected chapter, then each
of the children, and the baby-boy on his
knee repeats his after his father, and
finally each of the servants, down to the
last boy who has come in to black boots,
or to the Scotch sewing-lassie with her
broad accent. But how ennobling it is
for them all to take this audible part!

After breakfast our mother used to
read to us, and give us references to find
in our Bibles. We began, away back as
far as I can remember, with *Peep of Day*,
then *Line upon Line*, *Cobbin's Commentary*,
and so upward. In many cases I suppose the children of your families will go
to Sunday-school, instead of this home
Bible-class; but where it is so, let me
put in an earnest word in favor of the
young people meeting their parents, when
the school is over, and sitting beside them

during the service in the house of God.
If they sit with the Sunday-school children, the fidgetting around will be almost
certain to divert their minds; besides
which, most churches relegate the poor
children to the farthest and most uncomfortable parts of the building, — a distant gallery, with hard seats and high
backs, — as if little bodies never wearied,
and little minds didn't find it hard to
strain for the preacher's far-travelled
voice. What a reversal of matters would
take place if the Lord were to take direction! I believe he would send all the
people who occupy the best positions
packing from their comfortable seats,
which make them so drowsy, into the
uncushioned gallery, and call all the
happy children down to the best softly
cushioned pews, where he could keep

them well in sight, and hold their quick eyes fixed on his all the time.

If the father would let the boy sit next him, and find the places, and write the text out during the sermon, if he were too young to attend, and make a comfortable place for his head if he got sleepy; and if the mother could take the little girl's hand in hers, to say nothing of passing surreptitiously a little piece of sugar-candy to keep her from coughing (!), I cannot but think that those Sunday services would not be so great a weariness, but in after years would be recalled with pleasure by the lonely traveller in the backwoods, or the shepherd amid the Australian wolds.

In many cases the wife must stop at home and prepare the dinner, and, with a little management, a hot dinner need not take more time than a cold one. We always had a sirloin of beef and roast potatoes. Through a long course of years, without a single variation, that was so. Even now, when I eat sirloin of beef, especially the undercut, I have a kind of Sunday feeling. I remember that my father always had to turn the joint upside down, and that it was an exciting moment for us all, lest he should splash a drop of gravy over the clean cloth. If a drop did go over, my mother hastened, with a palliating excuse, and applied salt, for what reason I have not the remotest idea; but it served as a temporary expedient, and covered the mishap. These things may appear trivial, but they always were associated with Sunday, and that made them memorable.

Have plenty of singing on Sunday.
During the afternoon we read our books
or stories, but, as half-past four arrived,
we felt that the climax of the day had
come. My mother was not a pianist,
but she could just get through the tunes
of the old Psalmist; so she played, and
my father sat beside her, and sang with
his deep bass voice, and I stood beside
him and took the air, and my sister sang
too. We always had, " How sweet the
Name," " Guide me, O thou great Jeho-
vah " (to " Mariners "), and, very often,
" Around the throne of God in heaven,"
in memory of a little angel sister. Why
should not all the homes into which
this little volume comes start half-an-
hour's song-service each Sunday? But
the father and mother must themselves
take part.

Then tea; and after tea we said a
hymn all round; and, as I got older, I
was encouraged to read what I had
written of the morning sermon. And
so the blessed day passed to its close.
If old enough, there was the evening
service and supper (oh, the rapture of
sitting up to eat a potato in its jacket,
with a pat of butter inside, with pepper
and salt!). Again you say, very trivial,
and quite unworthy of occupying the
space here, or the time of the writer,
who, at fifty years of age, should care
for something better. Well, reader, you
may say what you like, but these simple things made Sunday the day of
days, and became the seeds which have
yielded harvests of content and blessed-
ness.

It is a mistake to gad about from one

minister to another. It begets a critical and captious spirit, and leads one to subordinate the worship of the sanctuary to the sermon. Find out the minister who, on the whole, helps you most, and the church which needs you most, and concentrate your time and thought on these. Never criticise the preacher before your children, and encourage them to remember and repeat what they can. Would that preachers would contrive to drop a few handfuls on purpose for the weary little listeners, whose eyes would glisten if *their* story were to be dropped into the discourse ; and the parents would be proud to explain that "our minister always thinks of the children."

It is very important that habits of reverence be inculcated in children.

"Why do I make you boys shut your

eyes in prayer?" asked a young lady of my congregation, of her class of ragged boys. Instantly two or three ragged arms went up, and one sharp youngster answered, —.

"To teach us manners, ma'am."

Was it not exactly true? The manners of the heavenly court are as exacting as those of the Queen's drawing-room, and it is well to begin early enough to inculcate them. Be in time at service; be reverent in your demeanor; take part in all you can; if you cannot sing, make a joyful noise; and never allow the Bible, or anything that belongs to God, to be made a subject for witticism in your presence.

Sunday company is, on the whole, to be eschewed. But, if friends drop in, ask them to fall in with your usual routine;

and with them, or in their absence, let
the conversation be tinctured, as far
as possible, with the spirit of the day.
My parents never talked familiarly of
God, but, somehow, there was a Sunday
air about the conversation; and certain
subjects, such as business, or pleasure-
seeking, or story-books, would seem in-
congruous. But there was no restraint,
no gloom, no Pharisaism, nothing irk-
some and tedious. To look happy, to
dress in our best, to sing, to talk cheer-
fully about all that interested us, this
was the high and happy key-note of our
family life on this best and brightest of
days.

Once more I crave indulgence if I
have been too personal in reciting these
remembrances of the past, but my motive has been at least innocent and trans-

parent ; for what has been may be done again, and it seemed better to photograph the dear old past than to produce a fancy picture which might seem rather a dream than a possibility.

X.

AMUSEMENTS.

X.

AMUSEMENTS.

THIS difficulty about amusements, where to go and where not to go, is not a new one. It agitated the Christians at Corinth centuries ago as it agitates us; and led up to one of those questions which the Apostle answered in his first epistle.

Dean Farrar, in his graphic style, explains the difficulty and perplexity of their position. They were daily living in the great wicked streets, in sight and hearing of everything that could quench spiritual aspirations and kindle carnal desires. The gay, common life pressed

on them so closely, the splendid vision
of Christ's advent seemed so far away,
might they not mingle with the heathen
festivals, join in the gay processions,
watch the dancing-girls, or take part in
the fun and frolic of the voluptuous city?
Were they to live always on the heavenly
manna, and never taste the onion, leek,
and garlic of Egypt? Were they never
again to drink of the foaming cup of
earthly pleasure, and mingle in the
dance, the feast, the pantomimic show?

In answer to these difficulties, the
Apostle laid down two principles, which
contain between them the very light *we*
need to enable us to pick *our* pathway
through the world, to teach us how to
act with regard to the thorny question
of amusements.

"All things are lawful for me, but not

all things are expedient: all things are lawful for me, *but I will not be brought under the power of any*" (1 Cor. vi. 12).

"All things are lawful, but all things are not expedient ; all things are lawful, *but all things edify not. Let no man seek his own, but each his neighbor's good*" (1 Cor. x. 23, 24).

We must have recreation, times when jaded nerves recuperate themselves, and tired brains turn from their absorbing thoughts to lighter themes. We shall perform the serious work of life more successfully if we have seasons of respite. We shall breast the Hill Difficulty more energetically after seasons of rest in the Arbor of Ease. Our many-stringed nature craves for seasons when laughter, song, and enjoyment may take the harp of life and sweep its lighter

chords.   And surely Nature's gayer
moods, when Spring scatters her flowers,
or Summer is ripening the year's produce, suggests, as Milton tells us in his
immortal *L'Allegro*, the relaxation of the
severer strain of business toil.   Little
children, with their ringing laughter,
their keen appreciation of mirth and
frolic, their demand for good times,
arouse us from our pensive melancholy
and laborious toils, quickening our
pulses, awakening our laughter, and
giving us an excuse, which we are not
loth to snatch, for casting aside the
serious business of life, and taking a
brief spell of pleasure.   Then the perpetual question arises, How far is all
this lawful and expedient? what should
be our attitude as Christians to amusement?   There are several principles to

guide us, but the ultimate decision must
ever remain with the individual; and it
is by our action on the debatable ground
of twilight, between the clearly defined
territories of absolute light or darkness,
that the most of us are made or marred.

First : *We must not be enslaved by any
form of pleasure.* The Apostle vowed
that he would not be brought under the
power of anything, however lawful or innocent it might be in itself.   It is marvellous how easy it is to become enslaved
to forms of pleasure-taking which in
themselves are perfectly harmless and
natural.   A man may be so intoxicated
with golf or cricket, a woman so fasci-
nated with lawn-tennis or bicycling, that
they are spoiled for all the practical business of life; and at the call of their
favorite pastime, will at any moment

renounce the most urgent and pressing engagements. It seems as if they can think, dream, and plan for nothing else.

When this is the case, whether the form of amusement be one of those healthy out-of-door pursuits already named, or the more hurtful absorption in the theatre, the ball, or the music-hall; when what should be only the means to an end becomes an end in itself; when we feel our best energies withdrawn from the serious demands of life, and dissipated in its flotsam and jetsam; when our soul is engrossed by the handling of a bat, the striking of a ball, the swiftness of a machine, — it is time to pull up and consider which way we are drifting. Surely life was given for higher purposes than these, and if it

be said that all such pastimes react on
the health and agility of the body, still
we must reply, that at the best the body
is only the organ and instrument of the
soul, and that it must be kept under
and made subservient to those lofty purposes which the soul conceives in its
secret place and executes in life's arena.

Next: *We must have an eye to others.*
There are forms of amusement which
we cannot indulge in without helping to
destroy the souls of others. They not
only do not build up, but they destroy
the work of God. We have no right to
jeopardize the eternal interests of those
who copy our example or who minister
to our enjoyment.

Paul says that, so far as he was con-
cerned, he felt at liberty to accept an in-
vitation to a meal in the precincts of an

idol-temple; but that he would not go lest the weak conscience of some fellow Christian should be defiled. Our attitude towards certain places of amusement and pastimes should be determined by our considering whether we would wish those who take their cue from our example to follow us thither. What effect will my conduct have on my children, my young brothers and sisters, the scholars in my Sunday-school class, and others who are not as strong as I am to resist the pernicious influences that are associated with this special form of amusement? Let me remember that young life is behind me, and though, as an experienced mountaineer, I might take the more precipitous route, for their sake I must follow the safe path.

Besides, we must consider whether the

effect of some system that gives us pleasure may not be in the highest degree deleterious in its effect on those who minister to our laughter or love of spectacular display. Have we any right, for our pleasure, to hold out baits of money to young girls or children or others, to jeopardize body and soul, and spend their days on the edge of the precipice? "All things edify not," said the Apostle, and we must seek not only our own but another's weal.

On the whole, *simple and natural pleasures are the best.* The skate over the frozen pond, rather than the dance in the over-heated ball-room; the family party, with its olden games, rather than the scenic representation of music-hall or theatre; the real rather than the artificial, the day rather than midnight, the dear ones of the home rather than the society of strangers. Let every one have a hobby; let every one become proficient in some branch of natural science or history; let every one do something well, be it to handle the oar or alpenstock, to use the camera, glide over the ringing ice, or climb the beetling crag. Let this man collect geological specimens, and that flowers or ferns, and that curiosities from various countries and people. But let there be some controlling interest, which shall give occupation in the summer ramble, or the snatch of foreign travel, and shall afford amusement in recollection, arrangement, and comparison, when the long winter evenings would hang heavily on hand.

Whatever does not leave a wry taste in our mouth, nor causes a feeling of

compunction and regret as we review it,
nor exerts a baleful effect on those who
minister to our enjoyment, nor unfits us
for prayer and communion with God,
nor so dazzles and blinds us that we can
find no pleasure in the simple delights
of home and natural beauty; whatever
is wholesome and health-giving; whatever is capable of being presented to
God in prayer as the object of his bless-
ing; whatever is in harmony with the
tender, holy, unselfish, and blessed nature of Jesus, — is an amusement which
we may gladly avail ourselves of; and
it shall be to us as the whetting of the
scythe amid the mower's toils, and as
the mending of the nets torn by the
midnight fishing-cruise.

XI.

THE USE OF THE SENSES.

XI.

THE USE OF THE SENSES.

OUR senses give warning signals when danger is near. This is perhaps their secondary use, but it is the most vital. The eye, ear, nose, the senses of taste and touch, are the channels through which the most exquisite pleasures are wafted to us — rapturous glimpses of natural beauty, sweet sounds, fragrant scents, delicious viands, and soft contacts; but they are also the avenues along which ride post-haste the couriers, warning of the approach of assassins that menace and imperil life. For the

most part what is inimical to health is
odious and distasteful to our senses, and
the quicker these become the more likely
we are to preserve the springs of life
from being poisoned and vitiated.

We are told in more than one Scripture, and notably in Heb. v. 14, that
there are spiritual counterparts to our
senses, and that we should exercise these
to discern good and evil. It is highly
important to do so; for as attention to
the warning of the physical senses will
preserve the health of our body, so attention to the warnings of our inner senses
will forewarn and forearm against the influences that are hostile to spiritual life.

Take the Ear of the Soul. In the case
of the savage the ear is trained to such
precision as to detect the footfall of a
stranger at an immense distance; and

in the case of the trained musician to discriminate between the most delicate shades of sound. Indeed, it would be impossible to train a singer for a place in the front rank of the profession whose ear was not extremely delicate and sensitive; and natural gifts in this direction may be still further trained to almost any degree of nicety. If the ear is not sensitive to the slightest discord, the voice can never be modulated to the finest harmonies.

And is there anything more necessary than to have the inner ear trained and exercised by contact with the Divine notes of an infinite charity! You may hear people talking most discordantly with this, criticising their neighbors, discussing their friends, uttering sharp and unkind judgments, all of which would be impossible if their ears had only been educated to detect the discords of their speech. ' But they talk on for years in utter oblivion of their false and dissonant notes. Amid so much discordance let us constantly seek for a pure ear, which will tell us in a moment when we have spoken a single word that is inconsistent with the perfect harmonies of the nature of God, which is love.

The Eye of the Soul. The eye detects the approach of danger, and, in the case of a savage, can do so in symptoms which are altogether meaningless to the ordinary vision. That bent blade of grass, that snapt twig, that almost imperceptible trail! Away on the mountain side the trained observer can see masses of troops where another finds only the shadows of passing clouds.

But the training of the eye of the soul is even more necessary, because it can anticipate the advent of temptation. It is bad when we have no warning of the stealthy approach of our worst adversary, till like a midnight assassin he has broken into the house of our life. Well is it when we can descry the gathering storm when it is still on the horizon, so as to reef our sails in time and be prepared for the squall ; when we can detect the pitfall before we come to it ; and see the brigand gang lying in wait before we reach the dark thicket; and anticipate complications and perplexities before we are amid them. By that clear prescience which is not the least of God's gifts we are the more likely to pass unscathed through life's ordeal because more able to appeal beforehand to Christ for succor.

The Scent of the Soul.   It is good to
have a keen sense of smell; it will save
us from many a noisome pestilence aris-
ing from the drain, or brooding in the
plague-laden air.   If it were not for this
invaluable gift, we might linger and
sleep amid deadly gases, unconscious of
the peril we were incurring.   It is well to
have this sense exercised.   I remember
once, after a voyage across the Atlantic,
visiting friends, who were spending
their summer holidays within a mile of
a sewage farm, the near neighborhood
of which was not noticeable to them,
but to which the pure ozone of the ocean
had made me extremely sensitive.

If our soul's sense of smell were more
keen, we should be quicker to perceive
when there was impurity in the speech or
behavior of our companions, and should

turn from them with disgust. The pure
lad would blush and hasten from the way
of the ungodly and the seat of the scorn-
ful. The highly spiritual and nobly tem-
pered woman would take no pleasure in
the double allusions of the music-hall, or
the highly spiced conversation of children of fashion. The pure in heart
would rush from the obscenity and oaths
with which too much of the talk of so-
called gentlemen is interlarded, as if
they had suddenly become aware of the
presence of an open sewer.

The Taste of the Soul. The sense of
taste sits as a sentinel at the entrance
of the alimentary canal to prevent hurtful and deleterious substances from en-
tering. How often has our first bite of
some fruit or food led us to eject it from
our mouth with disgust, thereby saving

our life! The rule is not invariable. There are substances which are most distasteful, but are nevertheless good as medicines, and palatable things are sometimes harmful to a degree; still, as a general rule, the palate may be trusted.

Now, how much evil might we be saved from, if only the taste of the soul were more highly educated in respect to the books which come into our hands. How often do young and inexperienced minds devour from beginning to end books, novels, treatises, which are highly inimical to their soul-life. If only they knew how to distinguish between good and evil, if only they could detect the subtle poison that had been instilled into those pages from the fangs of the great serpent, if only they were on the alert to reject that which blasts and blights the delicate growth of the better life, — how much suffering and consumption would be averted!

The Soul's Sense of Touch. The touch may be brought to an amazing degree of perfection, and become so sensitive that it can distinguish between the slightest variations in fabric or temperature. In members of the feline tribe — the cat or tiger — this sense is developed to its fullest perfection. But in man also it may become extremely acute.

Would that we might have that same sensitiveness to right and wrong, that we might with a touch be able to discern the one from the other, and have grace enough to accept the good and reject the evil. As the experienced hand can tell in a moment when a coin is light or not, so we might know whether a doctrine or statement tallied with the standard of God's truth or fell beneath it.

These distinctions are not to be learned in a moment. We may train our faculties from less to more ; by reason of use they may be exercised ; when the Spirit comes on us we shall, like our Master, be "quick of scent." But it is certain that we cannot long preserve the fine temper of the soul in such a world as this unless we carefully attend to the least monitions of the Divine Spirit operating through the senses of the soul.

XII.

CHRISTMAS.

XII.

CHRISTMAS.

HERE again! Welcome, thrice welcome! The darkest, shortest days of
the year are an appropriate season to
select for the Yule-log, the good cheer,
the home-gatherings, the presents and
gifts of young and old, which Christmas
brings!

The Yule-log! How we love it! For
ordinary days the coal-fire is good
enough; but, oh, the spluttering, the
crackling, the blue elfish flame of the
Christmas log! We need no candle or
gas-light, when the flame has caught it

in its lambent arms, and creeps along its edges, and eats into its heart. How hard that knot is fighting ! What a flare that resinous oil makes ! How sweet the scent, and fitful the light which rises and falls and flickers ! Now is the time to gather round for one brief hour of blessed, happy home-talk, between the lights — the light of the short winter day and the artificial light that must soon be brought in for the evening's work.

There should be no secrets in the family circle. The interests of each are those of all, and in the happy intercourse of the circle gathered round the flickering log, the common life gets illustrated and illuminated by quip and crank, by joke and tease, by the original saying of the little child, and the wise counsel of the father. It reminds me of those old mis-

sals, whose stern black letter-press is ac-
companied by the gorgeous margin, with
faces and figures, flowers and fruits,
dogs, monkeys, birds, and animals, friars
and monks, kings and queens, babes and
angels.

Happy are the children who are born
into large families. It is rare that an
only child reaches its fullest develop-
ment. There is a play, a reciprocal
influence, a chipping-off of corners, a
balancing, a taking-off of peculiarities, a
taking-down of pride, in a large family,
which are priceless. The children are
sure to pair off in twos, who will fight
for one another against the rest, and ex-
change endless confidences ; but, nevertheless, the interchange of repartee and
badinage between each with all will go
freely forward, and each member of the

family will appropriate spoils from the rest. Such free trade in one another's characteristics prospers best in the light of the Yule-log.

The Good Cheer! You tell me that there is waste and over-eating, and ask me to rebuke the busy housewives with their market-baskets and bargains, their turkeys, geese, plum-puddings, and mince pies. Well, of course, there should be no extravagance ; and we have no right to surfeit ourselves when the poor are starving at our doors. Before we sit down to our Christmas meals, we must provide portions for those that are without. Materials for good dinners must be sent to poor families who live in our immediate neighborhood, or our less prosperous relatives; the charwoman that comes once a week, the widowed mother of the boy

who brings the daily paper, the family of
the poor crossing-sweep, the respectable
old couple that are trying to keep themselves respectable and to avoid as long
as possible the workhouse, or the strug-
gling needlewoman whose customers will
not pay what they owe. Do not be
content with giving your guinea to the
church or parish fund, but find out the
needy and distressed, and with your own
hand minister to their need. And then,
with an easy conscience, you may sit
down to your well-spread board.

For my part, I like to see the butchers'
shops with the prize-meat, the poulterers'
with turkeys, geese, and chickens, hang-
ing in rich profusion, the pastry-cook
windows with their frosted cakes, and
the grocers' with their dried fruits and
candies, their teas and sugars, and all the

cunning enticements to mothers, sisters, wives, and daughters, to provide Christmas cheer. And then that great event in the housewife's year, the Christmas dinner! I like it, not of course for the rich and tempting dainties that resemble the fruit of the forbidden tree, in being pleasant to the eye and good for food; but because of the pleasure it gives the women of our homes in preparing it!

Such a vision of arms white with flour, and faces toasted by the fire, and whisperings over new recipes, and mysterious disappearances for hours together in the kitchen, of peeling, mincing, chopping, roasting, mixing, boiling, tasting, here comes over me, that I can but give myself up to congratulation for the opportunity that Christmas brings. Imagine the chance given to so many housewives for planning, scheming, arranging, purchasing, cooking, and serving, which are purely altruistic, of course. Free scope is given to so many unselfish qualities in the preparation of that great event of the year — the Christmas dinner !

The Home-Coming ! The boys and girls have come back from boarding-school ; and those who were fortunate enough not to go away to school have holidays. But this is not all. The eldest daughter, who has been absent the whole year in the distant town, is leaving by the night train, and will be here in the morning ; and the grown-up sons will bring their wives, and perhaps their babies; and the little midshipman will be back from the long and weary voyage. Oh, blessed festival of home, when the broken circles are formed again, and olden memories of the golden past are renewed. How many a life is kept sweet and pure amid the evil of the world, by the thought of the Christmas gathering, coming or passed !

How shall we gather up all the threads which the hours like swiftly gliding shutters weave ? Mother thinks that Mary looks rather over-wrought, and says so to the father, and they have a talk with her. She laughs merrily at their anxiety, and declares she is perfectly well, only tired with the Christmas rush. Then the father says he never saw the boys look so well, he is sure they have grown an inch, and he wants to know if their salaries have been raised. In the middle of the morning the sailor-boy arrives, and his mother kisses again and again the bronzed chubby face. In the afternoon the girls go round to see their girl-friends, not without a hope that their brothers will be at home; and the lads manage to come across the play-mates of their boyhood, whose faces have been their guiding stars through many a mile of tossing foam. Then dinner, and the old stories, the well-worn jokes, the reminiscences of what this one did or that in the old days, the babble of voices, the compliments to mother's cooking, the teasing of the sisters, their scathing answers, the happy, happy play of life and fun, till the whole party from the grandparents to the grandchildren have caught the infection. Oh, blessed English homes, the heart of old England can never grow old or sad so long as Christmas comes to stir your smouldering embers into flame !

The Gifts! For weeks before, there
have been schemings, whisperings, and
mysterious parcels brought in under
cloaks and secreted in safe places.
Hints dropped and caught at ! Leading
questions suggested ! Shops ransacked !
Purses emptied ! Probably each gets
back an equivalent for what he gives;
and probably also a good many things
are given which are of no kind of use.
Still, the thought for each other is lovely.
The endeavor to understand one another's needs is wholesome. And it is
always more blessed to give than to receive. What a wealth of giving has been
elicited by that Unspeakable Gift which
we commemorate at Christmas.

·Let us put no stint on our gifts, lest
the fountains of our life become frozen
at the heart. None would become a

Dead Sea, always taking in, and never giving out. But let us give, not only to those who can recompense us again, but to such as cannot repay.

Thus our Christmas days come and go. The happy party breaks up. We take our several ways, and settle to our pursuits. But the light of the Yule-log flickers still in our hearts, and the love of the home acts as a preservative against the evils of the world.

Do you know of lonely ones that have no Christmas circles awaiting them? Find them out, and invite them to join your own. Let there be with you, as with Israel, a tender thoughtfulness for the stranger that is within your gates. And be sure that all the Christmas joy is tinctured with the thought and love of God. Let the old family Bible be opened, and thanks be rendered to him of whom every family in heaven and earth is named. Let nothing be said or done to grieve his gentle and Holy Spirit. Let the home harmonies be keyed to those of heaven. And if there are the empty chairs, the vacant seats, the sad memories of vanished hands and silenced voices, look away to that great home festival in the many mansions of the Father's house, where the severed shall reunite, and the circles be complete, and from horizon to horizon shall be only love and peace and joy.